Sus *Sleuth Series*

The Mystery of the Tunnels
By Skye Oduaran

This is a work of fiction. Similarities to real people, places, or events are entirely coincidental.

THE MYSTERY OF THE TUNNELS

First edition. March 18, 2023.

Copyright © 2023 Skye Oduaran.
Written by Skye Oduaran.

Table of Contents

Prologue 5

Chapter 1 6

Chapter 2 13

Chapter 3 19

Chapter 4 28

Chapter 5 31

Chapter 6 34

Chapter 7 36

Chapter 8 41

Chapter 9 48

Chapter 10 50

Chapter 11 52

Chapter 12 57

Chapter 13 61

Chapter 14 64

Chapter 15 68

Chapter 16 72

Chapter 17 75

Chapter 18 84

Chapter 19..**88**

Chapter 20..**94**

Chapter 21..**99**

About the Author...**103**

Prologue

The night was dark, cold, and rainy. Lightning flashed, and thunder roared. However, inside the Himmington Palace, in the Kingdom of Sheffingham, all was quiet…except for the not-very-quiet activity in the secret vault.

The night guard was making his nightly rounds when he heard banging in the secret vault, lost in the sound of the thunder. In his curiosity, he decided to check what was going on…

Chapter 1

Standing in the vault, twelve-year-old, curly-haired Susie Cinnamon stared at the purple-and-red pillow, which was empty. The prime minister and butler stood around Susie, looking at her expectantly. The night before, the guard had heard a banging in the vault but could not open it as someone had locked it from the inside. That morning, the vault magically opened - it was no longer locked!

When the prime minister had gone inside to ensure everything was in the vault, like he did every morning, he found that the Golden Goblet, a valuable treasure, was gone. Stolen!

"It must have been an inside job," Susie Cinnamon said. She had three reasons to believe this:

Evidence A - The vault had been locked from the inside, and few would have known how to lock it like that.

Evidence B - The vault was secret and hard to find. It was behind a moving wall. There was a secret switch behind a painting on the wall. Flipping the switch moves the wall, revealing the vault.

Evidence C - The halls were dark, so the thief would have needed to find the vault with no light. This evidence indicates that the thief knew the secret vault's location.

Susie looked closely at the pillow and the indent the Golden Goblet had left. "As you may know," began the prime minister, "we are having a large ball here at the palace. We do not want any guests to learn about the theft."

Just as the prime minister finished speaking, a loud crash came from the upstairs room above the vault, interrupting Susie's thoughts. Susie immediately raced out of the vault and up the grand staircase. She burst into the lavishly furnished room above the vault, a space designed for leisure. A servant named Samuel Hardie lay sprawled on the floor, a rug on top of him. Hardie struggled to pull himself out from under the heavy rug as Susie entered. Seeing Susie, he stood up and dusted himself off. He was one of the shortest servants with a stocky build. His blond hair, disheveled from the rug, drew Susie's attention to the unusual brightness of his green eyes.

"Someone knocked me over from behind and threw a rug over my head.", said Hardie.
"Why would someone want to knock you over like that?" Susie inquired.

On an impulse, she looked up at the wall. Over 50 paintings hung close together. However, there was a gap between the two paintings in the middle of the wall. The markings on the wall announced that a picture had been hanging there recently.
"What painting used to be there?" Susie inquired.
Samuel Hardie gasped. "Only the most valuable painting in the kingdom!" he screamed.
"How much was it worth?"
"About $1,000,000,000!"
Susie gasped!
Another theft!
"Was it there before someone knocked you down?" Susie asked.
"Yes!" Samuel Hardie replied.
Who was the thief?
Did the thief knock Hardie over to steal the painting?
Why was the painting not protected?
How did the thief get the painting out of the room?

Staring at the empty gap, Susie suddenly had an idea. Maybe, the thief didn't escape yet!

The thief could be hiding in one of the adjoining rooms, waiting for a chance to escape. Putting a finger to her lips, indicating to Samuel Hardie to be quiet, Susie slipped into the adjacent room. Taking in her surroundings, Susie realized that the thief could be hiding in that particular room. Although it was small, it had good hiding places. It had a large, fancy bed, an ornate dresser, elegant curtains, and a closet. Quietly, Susie searched behind the curtains and the dresser, under the bed, and in the closet. There was no one hiding in the room.

Susie re-entered the room from which the thief had stolen the painting, where Hardie was still standing, perplexed at all that had just transpired. Susie searched the next adjoining room to find no one hiding in it. She searched two more rooms but still did not find any clues, not even the slightest clue. Susie knew that there was only one room left. Cautiously, Susie opened the door and entered the room. It was dark, with old statues covered with old, flowing silk cloths. It had only a tiny, high-up window. Any thief would hide in here, she thought to herself! It was quiet, dark, and still; there was not the slightest bit of movement.

Painstakingly, Susie searched the room, looking for any trace of the thief. She proceeded very quietly until she reached the back, right corner. The largest statue was standing there, and Susie detected a very slight movement underneath the unevenly draped cover of the statue. Was there something extra underneath the silk cover? Susie wondered to herself as she curiously crept toward the figure. Suddenly, her feet slipped out from underneath her, as she tripped on a silk cloth cover lying on the ground. Susie fell with a loud thud that echoed throughout the room. She looked up and saw that the cover for the most prominent statue was now sitting on the statue's figure, lopsided. The shape of the statue under the cover was different now!

Susie heard the sound of thudding feet racing away! She jumped up, exited the room, and began pursuing a fleeing figure through the empty hallway…

Chapter 2

The figure was dressed in a black cloak and wore black stockings that covered their feet. The person, probably the thief, was on the heavier side. They covered their face and hair with a black cloth so only their eyes showed. When the figure glanced back, Susie saw that the thief's eyes were light blue.

The figure reached the end of the hallway, where the only possible escape was a window with fancy drapes. Susie was about to catch up with the thief when the thief tore the drapes down and flung them over her. The drapes wrapped around Susie. They were heavy, and she could not free herself from them. She heard the cloaked figure run in the opposite direction down the hallway. Susie knew she had lost the criminal but was determined not to give up. First, she needed to escape the heavy curtain - before she ran out of air. After several minutes of struggle, Susie found an opening and freed her head first. Then, she twisted her left arm through the space, made it bigger, and freed her right hand. Afterward, she untangled her legs and stood up. Pushing the curtain to the side, Susie decided to check out the dark room again. Maybe the mysterious figure had left a clue.

Retracing her steps to the back, right corner of the room, Susie inspected the floor. She did not see anything promising. Susie glanced up at the statue with the lopsided covering and, with a swift movement of her hand, pulled the cover off. Cobwebs and dust formed a cloud engulfing Susie as the silk cloth fell to the floor. Brushing off the dust and webs that covered her, Susie looked at the statue. It was a statue of the former king, Quincy Everboken III, who had lost his position as king because of suspicion that he had masterminded a massive bank theft. His cousin, John Topps, a well-liked king, known for his honesty and integrity, replaced him.

Susie continued to examine the statue. Nothing unusual. From the corner of her eye, she saw a gleaming object on the ground. She found something! At the base of the statue was a small coin made of solid gold, with the image of a hawk on the backside. It was pressed down and distorted on the front side, so she could not make out what was on it.

Susie decided to inquire around the palace about the coin before returning to the vault to continue her investigation. She began her questioning with Samuel Hardie. As soon as Hardie saw the golden coin, a funny look flashed across his face. Was it surprise, panic, or recognition? Susie was not sure.

"Have you seen this before?" Susie asked suspiciously.
"What?- Uh, no?" came the reply.
"Are you sure?" Susie inquired.
"Well, I believe that the hawk was the symbol of former King Everboken III, but I am not absolutely sure."

Next, Susie interviewed the prime minister. He was a tall, thin man with dark brown eyes. "No, I have never seen that coin before, but that one may be old, and I just started working here."

Since many guards were around the palace, Susie decided to save time and only inquire with the guard who had heard the banging in the secret vault. "Hmmm… yes! That is the coin of former King Everboken III. I used to be the top guard during his reign."

Perhaps it was not very unusual that Susie found the golden coin in the room. It was with the statue of former King Everboken III, and the other artifacts were probably of things from his reign. Susie would check this out later. After all, the coin may well be insignificant to the mystery.

Afterward, Susie interviewed the butler. He was a stout, heavier man with blue eyes, blond hair with brown highlights, and a chiseled chin. "No... I have never seen this coin before.", was his answer to Susie's inquiry.

Susie returned to the dark room filled with covered statues. She pulled the cloth off the figure closest to her. The statue was of King Everboken III's queen, Tiffany the Good-Hearted. Over the next hour, Susie uncovered and examined all the statues. They were all from the reign of King Everboken III. She wondered why the coin was there when no other relics from Everboken III's reign besides statues were in the room. Susie decided to search the secret vault of the Golden Goblet for clues and worry about the coin later. She would check the archives and library of the palace to pick up any helpful information about the golden coin when she had the opportunity.

Chapter 3

Susie hurried downstairs because she knew that with every moment that passed, the thief was getting away and would eventually hide all traces of their existence. As she reached the bottom of the grand stairway, Susie checked to ensure no one was around to see her open the vault. It was secret; she reminded herself. No one was around, so she flipped the switch behind the painting, and the wall moved aside. Susie stepped through, and the wall slid back into position. Darkness immediately enveloped Susie.

Digging in her pocket, Susie found a battery-powered light. Switching it on, she discovered a solid steel wall in front of her, with a small metallic door in the middle. Susie decided to check the lock. It did not appear that it had been tampered with, which supported her suspicions that the thief had a key. Even before examining the lock, she figured the thief would not have picked the lock because there was an alarm system. Perhaps the alarm system was tampered with before picking the lock. However, she told herself, the alarm system might as well be inconsequential as the lock had shown no signs of tampering.

Could the thief have done an excellent job, leaving no evidence of tampering with the lock? If so, the thief must have been experienced and had done things like this many times before.

Susie realized that speculation would not solve the mystery. She needed to figure out how the alarm system worked in the first place. She decided to get one of the palace repairmen to look at it, and she would go from there. Susie turned her back to the metallic door and looked at the place where the moving wall was. She felt around that area until she found a round hole. Sure enough, it was a tiny keyhole! Just what she was looking to find. Someone could lock the moving wall from the inside by inserting a key into the hole. But, the keyhole took a lot of hard work to find. How did the thief know that the keyhole was there? There were two possible ways, as far as Susie could figure:

> 1.) The thief was good at finding things that were unseen or in hidden places.
> 2.) The thief knew the vault well, indicating an inside job or an accomplice from within the palace.

Susie looked next to the keyhole. There was also a switch to get the wall to move. She flicked the switch, and the wall moved aside. Susie stepped out and turned off her flashlight. The wall closed silently behind her. Susie began walking down the hall towards the prime minister's office to inquire about finding one of the palace repairmen.

Susie knocked on the prime minister's office door and entered. The prime minister was seated at his desk. He looked up. "What can I do for you, miss?"

"I would like to know where I can find a repairman so they can look at something." Everyone could be a possible suspect, so Susie had decided to be vague in telling about her progress and what she had found out. However, why would the prime minister rob the palace, anyway? He was the one who had called her to come to solve the mystery. Additionally, Susie could not identify any possible motive as he had a good position at the palace and was wealthy.

"Is something broken?" the prime minister asked.
Susie decided that it would be okay to tell him. "I would like to have a repairman look at the alarm system of the secret vault."
"Oh, that is quite alright…I believe that Timothy Robins is on his break. You may check the east side of the palace grounds, near the pond, where he is always on his break." The prime minister tapped his fingers together.

Susie, all of a sudden, was distracted. There was a black cloak on the wall. Was it the same one worn by the figure she had pursued? Was the prime minister the thief? Susie knew that she needed to keep an open mind. People's actions can surprise you.

The prime minister followed Susie's gaze to the cloak.
"Sir, may I ask you, is that cloak yours?"

"No, I was wondering how it got there. Perhaps a maid hung it there".

Susie thought for a moment. It looked a lot like the cloak the thief had worn. Why was it in the prime minister's office? Was the prime minister being set up? Susie pulled it down from the wall and inspected it. The prime minister was tall and thin, and Susie saw that the tailoring of the cloak was for a small, stout man. That supported what the prime minister had said. It made Susie more suspicious that someone was setting him up. But why him?

"I believe I will hold on to this.", Susie announced.

She thanked the prime minister, then walked outside. The east side of the palace grounds held a large pond. Marble benches decorated the perimeter. A broader man with a red beard and bright blue eyes sat relaxing on a marble bench across the pond. Walking around the pond took Susie around 15 minutes. As Susie approached, the man stood up.

"Sir, are you Timothy Robins?" Susie asked.
"Yes, miss. What can I do for you?"
"I would like for you to look at the alarm system of the secret vault."
"Well… my break is almost over, so we can go now."
Susie followed Mr. Robins back to the palace.
While they were walking, Susie took notice of Mr. Robins' figure. He was stout enough to fit in the cloak.
"Excuse me, but does this cloak happen to belong to you?" Susie showed the cloak from the prime minister's office to Mr. Robins.
"No, I have never seen it before," he said in a tone that seemed to evade the question.

In a few minutes, Susie and Mr. Robins reached the vault. Susie flipped the switch, and the wall moved. Mr. Robins began to examine several wires. "I see that someone cut one of the wires. You can tell because of how clean the edge of the wire is."

That would be how the thief had avoided the alarm going off!

After Mr. Robins left, Susie decided now would be a perfect opportunity to check out the actual vault, past the metallic door. Susie obtained a key from a guard down the hall. She re-entered through the moving wall and used her flashlight to find the keyhole beside the metallic door. Susie inserted the key and slipped through the short doorway. On a podium was the red-and-purple pillow that had once held the Golden Goblet. The room was small, and Susie began to search it. While searching, she accidentally stepped on something. Bending down, Susie found a knife. Was this how the thief had cut the wire?

Chapter 4

Okay, Susie said to herself as she gathered her thoughts. How did the thief escape the vault? Did the thief go out using the moving wall or…is there another way out? Susie began feeling the walls. She also tapped them to see if they were hollow. Unfortunately, she found nothing.

Then, Susie had an idea. She began tapping the floor until she found a hollow spot. There was a small crack near the hollowed-out area. Could the thief have peeled up the floor? Susie began to edge her nails under the gap. She had to work on this for a while, but eventually, she managed to pry out a metal piece of the floor. Susie tried to set it down gently, but it was heavy, and the metal panel hit the floor with a loud bang! That was probably the banging the night guard had heard! Susie picked up her flashlight from where she had set it while prying up the floor. She shone it down the hole.

The flashlight revealed a secret set of stairs directly under the vault. Susie quietly crept down them. When she reached the bottom, she saw many tunnels running in different directions before her. There were at least six. Susie wanted to explore all of them, but where to start? She decided to begin with the one to the far right. Do all these tunnels lead under the palace grounds? She wondered to herself. Susie began to walk down the tunnel. It was filthy, and a mouse would skitter across every now and then.

Susie suddenly stopped after about 10 minutes. She thought she had heard a set of footsteps. Was it a mouse? Listening, Susie heard the footsteps behind her - someone was following her! Who was it? The footsteps began to get closer. Susie started to run! The footsteps behind her got faster and faster. Susie followed the tunnel. She saw that the tunnel ahead split into two different ones. Susie stopped running for a second. Which way should she go?

Chapter 5

Susie rapidly began to think. All the while, the footsteps got nearer and nearer. Suddenly, she had an idea!

Susie crept into the tunnel that branched off to the left and turned off her flashlight. Susie took off the pearl necklace that she wore around her neck. She threw it into the opposite tunnel, the one branching to the right, making it seem like she was in it. Susie heard the footsteps of her pursuer slow and go into the tunnel toward where Susie had thrown the necklace. The footsteps then quickened. Susie removed her shoes and began carrying them so her footsteps would be quiet. Susie ran after the person in the tunnel. She was very curious about who the person was, but decided to keep her flashlight off so the person who had chased her would not know she was following them. Was the person she was chasing the thief?

While running quietly in pursuit of the figure, Susie realized the ground was dusty. She paused momentarily to look at the dirt. There were footprints ahead of her left by the figure she was chasing. A heavier person made them. Susie could tell by how deeply set the prints were. She decided to continue moving forward rapidly to keep an eye on the person ahead of her.

Susie remembered that the cloak she had obtained from the prime minister's office would only fit a stout, short man. The footprints also appeared to be made by someone heavy. Who was heavy, stout, and short in the palace? Susie knew of four people: the butler, Timothy Robins, Samuel Hardie, and one of the guards. Susie continued moving on. She heard the other person's footsteps in the distance and began to speed up. Susie could soon sense that the thief was no more than a few feet away and slowed down. Suddenly, the person ahead of her stopped. Susie immediately froze, hardly daring to breathe.

Chapter 6

"I guess that girl got away. Never mind, I'll prevent her from catching me yet.", the person ahead of her said. Susie could not tell whose voice it was, but it was male.

Susie heard the footsteps continue and followed them, leaving a bit more space between her and the man. After about 30 minutes, the person ahead of Susie took a turn and came to another staircase. The person mounted the stairs and started pushing an object above his head. From the sound of what he was doing, Susie could tell that he was trying to push up the floor of a room. Suddenly, light illuminated the staircase and the tunnel as the man pushed up the trap door. Susie saw that the man who had chased her was climbing out of the tunnel.

Susie figured the man who climbed out of the tunnel was the thief. He was wearing black stockings and shiny black shoes. He was a short, stout man with a black fabric over his head. There was only a small opening for his eyes, which were blue. The man was not wearing a black cloak, as he had earlier that day. Susie assumed it was because she still had it in her possession. In the absence of the cloak, Susie could see that the thief was wearing a blue and silver uniform with a matching pair of knickerbockers. The uniform looked familiar. Where have I seen it before? Susie asked herself. After the thief finished climbing out of the tunnel, he placed the floor back in. Susie waited a few seconds, then climbed the stairs. She tried to push the trap door up but found it did not budge.

Chapter 7

Susie heard laughing above her.

"I have caught you now! I placed a heavy chair above you so you cannot push the floor up! Now that you are stuck, you cannot catch me as I continue stealing and selling precious objects! And I'm sure you do not know where another opening is. Even if you find one, I won't be waiting for you!"

Susie did not recognize the voice but could tell it was not joking. She needed to find a way out of the tunnels!

Susie pushed and shoved on the floor above her. The thief had chosen a heavy chair! She climbed down the staircase and turned on her flashlight. Susie started to follow the tunnel to where a fork was. Once she reached it, she took a new tunnel. Susie followed it for several minutes until her flashlight ran out of battery. Susie stumbled in the darkness, keeping one arm on the tunnel's wall. Suddenly, she tripped on a ledge going upwards and fell to the ground. Susie stood up and carefully followed the tunnel as it climbed upwards. Before long, Susie reached a small door. She pushed it, and, to her relief, it swung wide open. Instantly, light poured in from outside and illuminated the tunnel. Susie stepped out from the tunnel through the wide-open door into the fresh air. She saw that she was now standing outside. Taking in her surroundings, Susie saw that the tunnel led into a man-made cave by a river. Turning around, Susie glanced at the door she had just passed through. It was hardly visible, and the only evidence of the door being there were two rusted metal hinges. She tried to push the door inwards, but apparently, opening the door was only possible from the other side.

Susie turned around with her back to the cave and gazed at the river and surrounding woods. She knew a river flowed past the palace's east side, presumably where she was. There was a path leading through a wood, with the palace turrets visible in the distance. Susie had clearly followed the tunnel a very long way. She began to walk down the path. It took a while before Susie made it to the palace. Susie found that all the palace guards had gathered together when she arrived. One thing immediately caught Susie's attention: all the guards wore blue and silver uniforms. They also had matching knickerbockers, black stockings, and shiny black shoes, just like the thief had worn! A guard may be the thief!

Then, her eyes landed on one guard in particular. He was stout, with blue eyes. All the other guards were noticeably thinner than him. Was *he* the thief? He certainly fit the person she saw in the tunnels. However, he appeared considerably taller than the thief, although it may have been her imagination.

Not wanting to interrupt the meeting of the guards, Susie decided to check the archives and library. On the way, she passed the butler, who politely said hello. Susie thought it was strange that his hair had appeared pressed down. All workers in the palace were required to be presentable. Susie watched as the butler entered the bathroom, maybe to fix his hair. Susie continued to the library, not giving the butler another thought.

After a brief search, Susie found a book about King Quincy Everboken III. There was a portrait of him included in the book. He was very familiar with a somewhat chiseled chin, blond hair with little dashes of brown, and blue eyes. Susie thought for a moment but could not remember where she had seen someone who looked like that.

Next, Susie looked at a book about recent coins. She searched for the golden coin she had found and located it on page 239. It perfectly matched the coin she had discovered earlier. The minting of this coin was at the request of King Everboken III himself to honor his reign.

Susie continued to ponder where she had seen the face of King Everboken III before. It was highly familiar, and it nagged at Susie's mind. Susie had seen that face before, but this was the first time she had looked at a picture of the former king, who had reigned before she was born. Susie was sure that she had seen someone like this not too long ago…

Chapter 8

That evening, it began to rain. At 7:00 PM, Susie, the prime minister, the butler, and the maids sat at the long mahogany table in the dining room to discuss the recent thefts and plans for the fancy ball the next day. The electric chandelier above them was the only thing that lit the room.

Suddenly, the chandelier began to flicker. Within moments, all of the lights in the palace went out! The entire palace plunged into pitch-black darkness!

At first, everyone sat in silence, hoping the lights would come back on. When it was apparent that the lights would not return for a while, everyone in the room started talking at once.

Susie heard people say, "What is going on?", "Why did the lights go out?" and "Is there a storm?"

Ten minutes later, the lights flickered back on. There was a scream from the adjoining kitchen. The head chef came running into the dining room.

"The rare and most priceless China plates in the kingdom are gone! Someone stole them when the lights went out," she exclaimed.

How many thefts will happen in less than 24 hours? Susie wondered as she jumped up and ran into the large kitchen. Susie asked the head chef where she kept the plates.

The head chef led her to a metal cabinet with a large lock.

"I believe that the lights going out was no coincidence. Someone may have turned out the lights so they could come in and steal the plates.", Susie said.

Susie looked at the lock. It was intricate and required a key. Susie returned to the dining room and asked the prime minister who had keys to the cabinet in the kitchen. "Only the butler, the top guard, the head chef, the duke, and myself have keys. The duke is away on a business trip."

Susie turned and looked at the table. The butler sat there as still as a stone… he had the same features Susie saw in King Everboken III's portrait. Chiseled chin, blond hair with brown highlights, blue eyes, heavy figure… The butler *is* King Everboken III! What was he doing here? Was *he* the thief?

Susie knew she couldn't just assume he was guilty because he was working here. She needed to gather evidence against him. And he was at the table during the most recent theft. He could not have left the table because he was sitting directly across from Susie. If he was a thief in one of the earlier thefts, he must have had an accomplice…

The butler had also lied about the coin. Why did he pretend he had never seen it before if he requested the palace make the coin in his honor? Furthermore, Susie saw that his hair had been pressed down earlier. The thief in the tunnel had worn a fabric over his head. If the butler was the thief, the fabric might have pressed his hair down, and he entered the bathroom to fix it. But how could he be the thief if the thief in the tunnel wore a guard's uniform?

"Are there any other valuables in this palace that might be the next target?" Susie wondered out loud.

"I can think of four most important valuables," responded the prime minister. "The Kriston Sapphire, the Perry Montix painting, the golden crown, and, most importantly, *The Most Important Treasure In The Whole Country*." The prime minister emphasized the last bit and lowered his voice. The Most Important Treasure In The Whole Country must be exceptional and priceless. The prime minister said he would show them to her the next day.

Susie then went to the palace basement and found a repairman she had never met before examining the electrical system.

"Do you know what happened?" Susie asked.

The repairman looked up and said, "I see that someone has turned off the electricity, which is common knowledge. It only requires flipping a simple switch."

Susie thanked him and returned upstairs. When she returned to the dining room, she saw the butler was gone. "He went to arrange some plans for the big ball tomorrow.", a maid said when Susie asked.

Nothing sounded suspicious about that, but Susie just wanted to make sure. She peeked through the small window of the butler's office and found him looking over several papers and writing things down.

As she walked away, Susie began to think. The big ball tomorrow would be the perfect distraction to pull off another theft because everyone in the palace would attend the ball. So, during the ball, Susie would make rounds around the palace and check on all the valuables while everyone was at the ball. Susie knew that no guests at the ball could learn about the thefts.

Susie entered a sitting room and sat down. There was a newspaper on the coffee table in front of her. She picked it up. The headline on the front page read, "GOLDEN GOBLET STOLEN FROM HIMMINGTON PALACE!"

Chapter 9

Someone in the palace had leaked that information! Susie knew this because only the people in the palace knew of the thefts. She decided to call the reporter and ask who provided the information relating to the robbery. Susie was not sure that she would come up with anything because journalists do not usually reveal their sources.

It was rather late, so Susie would call the reporter the next day.
Taking her coat off of the coat rack, Susie began putting it on. As she was buttoning it, she felt something on the inside pocket. Reaching inside, Susie removed a piece of paper, unfolded it, and found the following message written in red pen:
STOP LOOKING INTO THE THEFTS, OR ELSE.

Apparently, the thief was getting desperate, desperate enough to threaten her. However, Susie was not afraid. She began to walk through the dim hallway towards the front door. Susie was passing by a big dark room. She stopped all of a sudden because she thought that she saw a figure inside! Susie curiously peered in through the doorway. She watched as the figure walked up to a display case, lifted his arm, and swung it swiftly at the glass case with what appeared to be a hammer. The hammer slammed into the case with a resounding bang, and the case shattered into smithereens! Shards of glass rained down over the polished oak floor!

Chapter 10

Susie still kept peeking through the doorway. The figure picked up a gleaming object and placed it in the pocket of his black trousers. The thief was stealing a precious object while everyone else in the palace was working on the ball plans!

As the thief approached the doorway, Susie pressed herself up against the wall, hoping she would not be seen. The thief walked out of the room, turned, and continued down the hallway. He entered another room. All this time, Susie was shadowing the thief. She entered the room and hid behind an oversized chair. Susie watched as he peeled up a panel of the polished wooden floor. What was he doing? Maybe there was another tunnel below the floor. She needed to stop the thief. Susie jumped up from her hiding place and shouted, "Stop!"

The thief saw Susie and shoved the wood panel back into the floor. Susie was near the door, and as the thief ran to get out, Susie tripped him. She looked closely at the fallen thief, who turned out to be…

Chapter 11

…Samuel Hardie! Susie immediately called for the guards to come. Three came immediately.

"Fine," Hardie admitted. "I helped with a few thefts here and there and was stealing the Varchirer Diamond-encrusted Slate, but I will not tell you who else is involved in our heists until our final project is done!" Susie knew she had caught one thief, but there were more.

"Just one question," Susie began. "Is the butler involved in any way?"
"I will not tell you anything!" Samuel Hardie said. Susie knew she would need to find the other thief or thieves and stop them tomorrow!

The next day, Susie returned to the palace. Everyone was busy decorating and setting things up for the ball. Susie went to the telephone and called the reporter, Caroline Tram, who had written about the Golden Goblet theft. Just as she thought, the reporter would not reveal her sources.

Susie left the telephone and located the prime minister. He began to show her around the left wing of the palace. The ball was to be on the right wing, so the thief would probably not get caught, as they would be in the wing opposite of the ball. The sapphire was behind a moving shelf. The crown was behind a secret panel of the wall. The small painting hung on the expansive wall with many other pictures, all the same size. Susie thought of it as a lousy hiding place, but it was near the ceiling, and you would need a ladder to reach it.

Finally, the prime minister showed Susie The Most Important Treasure In The

Whole Country. It was very securely locked. A shelf would rotate after you push back one of the heavy books on it to trigger the mechanism, and you had to step on the shelf's frame to go to the side that was not visible. Then, you needed to unlock 5 locks and enter a secret password to open the titanium metal doors on the other side of the shelf. Through that door was another set of titanium doors. You had to enter a long password. If it was incorrect, even by one single digit, an alarm would sound, and a guard would come to see who was in between the set of doors. If you entered the password correctly, you would end up in a bright room with solid titanium metal walls. The floor was made of several panels of steel. A large safe sat in the center of the room. The safe required several combinations, a password, and a key.

The prime minister did not open the safe for Susie, leaving her to guess what was inside. The prime minister had Susie memorize all the passwords and handed her all the keys except for the one that opened the safe. He said there were no spare keys, so Susie had to take care of them. They went through all the doors, and they all closed behind them. They stepped onto the rotating shelf and rode it until it halted. Susie put the keys immediately into the inside pocket of her jacket. Each treasure was in a different room, but they all branched off from a hallway that ended at a window. There was a fancy bench under the window, and Susie sat down, where she could see who entered the four rooms that held the valuables.

    Susie sat there for a long time. Half an hour turned into an hour, and an hour turned into two, then three, then four. Nothing took place. Susie stood up and went into the room with the painting. It was still there. She checked the room with the crown. It was also still there. Then, she inspected the room with the sapphire. Susie found the moving shelf, flipped a hidden switch, and the bookshelf slid aside. Susie checked the hole in the wall where the sapphire was supposed to be…

Chapter 12

It was gone! It was there when the prime minister showed it to her, and afterward, she sat watching the entrances to all the rooms for four hours! How could the sapphire have been stolen? Susie heard and saw nothing.

A sudden thought struck Susie: what if The Most Important Treasure In The Whole Country was stolen?! Susie rushed out into the hallway. She immediately ran into the room where The Most Important Treasure In The Whole Country was kept.

Susie went through all the locks and passwords and reached the set of doors requiring one long password. In her haste, she made a mistake, and the alarm sounded. A guard came rushing immediately, only to find Susie had put in the wrong code.

Susie reported the theft of the sapphire. The guard went and looked at where it had been and admitted that he could do nothing. "You were sent here to find the thieves of our palace valuables," he said.

Susie returned to the room where the sapphire was stolen from as the guard returned to his post. Susie had a sudden idea and looked at the floor. It was made of marble panels with intricate designs painted on the edges. Susie tried to pry each one up from the floor and found that she could remove one wide enough for her to fit through. Before going in, she chose a candle from a holder in the room and went through the hole and down a flight of stairs. At the bottom of the stairs was the dusty floor. Susie saw a set of footprints that were hard to make out. They were of a light person, probably a man from the looks of it. It appeared that the person had a long stride. From the size of the prints, the person who had left them was tall. A lot of the guards at the palace were tall, and so was the prime minister.

Susie understood that she must remain unbiased in solving the mystery. But, she suspected that the prime minister was being set up, and he was the one who had called her to help. Two cooks in the kitchen were tall, as were at least ten servants in the palace.

Susie began to follow the prints down the tunnel and realized it was connected to other tunnels. Susie figured an extensive network of tunnels ran under the palace and its expansive grounds. The thief used the tunnels to get into the room with the sapphire, stole the jewel, and got away. Perhaps that could happen with all the other treasures, too! Susie was alarmed by this idea.

Susie followed the prints to a fork where the tunnel split and chose the left one because it was the one the footprints followed. Susie spotted a shiny object on the ground as she started down the left tunnel.

It was a golden pen with the letters Z.W. carved on the side. Why was the engraved pen down here? Was the Z.W. someone's initials? Susie slid it into her pocket for later.

Chapter 13

Susie continued to follow the footprints. She had to pay close attention to ensure she kept track of the prints because it was so dusty and dim, and mouse tracks would sometimes interfere. At one point, she could not even see the footprints, and it took her several minutes to find them again, and by then, her tracks had messed them up. Nevertheless, Susie went on following the prints some more.

After following the tracks for a little while, the footprints completely vanished. Susie looked all over the ground, but there was no trace of the prints. They were completely gone! She lifted the candle and looked at the roof of the tunnel. It was made of solid cement. There were the markings of a circle that was darker than the cement around it. Susie pushed on the circle above her but could not push it up.

Was it the floor of another room? Susie felt around the edges and found a switch. Susie immediately flipped it, and the circle above popped out. After a few minutes of struggle, Susie managed to pull herself out of the tunnel. Once she was out of the hole, Susie realized she was in the palace's cellar. Susie found a switch on the musty ground next to the circular hole. She flipped it, and the circular cover filled the hole once more.

  Suddenly, the candle went out, but not before Susie could glimpse around the room. It was filled with lots of jars and boxes. Because Susie had left her electric light at home and had no matches, she had to feel around in the dark until she found the stairs. Finally, she found them.

  Because she had no light, she had to be extremely careful as there was no railing. The stairs were made of smooth marble, were steep, and to a certain extent, crumbling. Twice she slipped and almost fell down the stairs.

    Once she reached the top, she found a landing to step onto. Standing on the platform, she saw a cement wall before her. She had to squint in the dark but finally found a switch on the wall. She flicked the switch, the wall slid over, and Susie stepped out into bright light.

Chapter 14

Susie was in the large kitchen of the palace. The kitchen was busy with lots of staff because of the big ball. Susie approached the nearest cook and asked if anyone had come out of the cellar in the past hour.

"Yes, one of the cooks, Mary Camere, went down there to get some cumin. I recall that the butler also entered. A servant named Zachem entered the cellar, too. I also believe that I saw the prime minister go in there.", came the reply.
"Why would the prime minister or butler enter the cellar?" Susie asked.
"I don't know.", said the cook.

Susie ran down the halls to the office of the prime minister. She entered and asked the prime minister why he had gone into the cellar. "I went into the cellar because I was looking for something but was unable to find it."

Susie then searched for the butler but was unable to find him.

Susie also went to see Zachem. The golden pen that Susie found in the tunnel had the letter Z on it. Further, Zachem was tall.

Zachem said he went down there because someone had seen mice in the cellar and wanted to look into it. There were no mice, only pieces of cotton. Susie also showed him the pen and asked if it was his. "No, however, I believe that the letters on it are the initials of the prime minister, Zachary Whitley.", came the reply.

Susie was beginning to suspect the prime minister because he was tall, and the initials on the pen matched his. If he was another thief and Susie brought the pen to him, he may suspect she was getting on his case. Susie did have an idea, though. She would ask others where he was from 12:00 PM to 1:00 PM.

Susie asked several maids, servants, and cleaners. Each one responded that they had never seen him since she had shown up. Maybe the prime minister really was the thief, and he stole the sapphire, followed the tunnels, and came out into the kitchen. His excuse of "looking for something" may have been a lie.

Susie peered into the prime minister's office. He was not inside. Maybe searching his office was a logical next move.

Susie opened every desk drawer until she came to one with a lock. Susie saw that it required a password. Many people create passwords based on events or people in their lives. Susie did not know much about the prime minister, so she started with something simple: ZACHARY WHITLEY.

The lock opened! This verified that his name was Zachary Whitley. Was he the thief, or was he being set up? If he was being set up, the real thief must have taken the prime minister's pen when he was not in his office and left it in the tunnel.

Susie opened the drawer and gasped!

Chapter 15

In the drawer was the sapphire! So the prime minister was the thief. Susie doubted that he was being set up now. He was tall and thin, and his stride was definitely long. She took a picture of the sapphire with a camera from her pocket. She also took a picture of the pen she had found in the tunnel. They were vital evidence. Susie also found a paper in the drawer. It said:

'Robins, I have learned that Samuel Hardie has been caught. We must take great care to ensure Susie does not figure it out. Our Final Project is waiting until the ball begins. Be prepared. I tricked that girl, so she is watching "The Most Important Treasure In The Whole Country." Really, the safe is locked but empty. Now she is occupied. The painting and the crown are fakes, too! She is busy watching those.

Last I saw her, she was sitting at the head of the hallway watching the rooms. So, I used the tunnels to steal the sapphire. She probably does not know. (I only stole the sapphire for my own enjoyment, knowing she expects to see me but can't. The sapphire is of little value compared to what we have stolen and what we will steal). Meet me near the cave entrance by the river, east of the palace, at 2:15.
     - Whitley'

    Susie took a picture of the paper, put it and the sapphire back into the drawer, and relocked it.

    Why leave the note inside the drawer instead of taking it? Susie queried. Perhaps Robins had yet to read the message, she thought.

    Susie was also shocked that the prime minister and Timothy Robins were the thieves. They had not seemed to be up to something like this. She looked at her watch. It was 1:52 PM.

Susie had a plan. She would hide and use her camera to record their meeting. Then, she would know what they were planning. The recording would also be evidence. Once she knew what they were up to, she could record them in the process of *The Final Project*, which would be her evidence for court. After this, she would catch them somehow…

Susie jumped up and went outside. It was 1:55, and Susie knew she had to get to the meeting place before the thieves. The cave by the river, which Susie discovered yesterday, was the meeting place. She ran as fast as she could, following an overgrown path beside the river. Susie thought that it was a shortcut.

She followed it for three minutes but was nowhere near the cave. Susie continued going over rocks and roots, and logs. It was 1:59! Susie had 16 minutes before the meeting but needed to get to the meeting spot before the thieves could. She stopped for a minute to untangle her leg from a vine. Her watch soon turned 2:00! Susie paused for a moment to take in her surroundings. She did not recognize the area. Maybe this was not a shortcut…

Chapter 16

Susie was lost! She decided to circle back the way she had come and take the paved path. Unfortunately, Susie had wandered away from the overgrown trail. She reminded herself that she was not lost, just misplaced.

It was now 2:03! Susie thought that the overgrown path was the older, longer route. Susie continued on until she saw an old wooden structure. She entered it out of curiosity, hoping that if there was someone inside, they could give her directions to the cave.

As she was entering, the floor cracked and sagged beneath her. It was unstable. No one was around. She carefully crossed the floor to the other side and found that the floor was stable again when she reached the far wall. Susie glanced at her watch. It was 2:05!

She left the structure and continued to wander. She was still near the river. Suddenly, she had an idea. She saw an old canoe made of wood nearby. She pushed it into the fast-moving water and jumped in. The river immediately pulled the canoe as fast as it could. Unfortunately, Susie did not see any paddles, so she could not steer around rocks.

Eventually, Susie saw the cave coming up. Swiftly, she grabbed a jagged rock near the shore and climbed out of the canoe, leaving the canoe to continue down the river without her. This would ensure that Robins and the prime minister would not know of her presence. She propped up her camera in a pile of rocks, making it invisible to the thieves. Because the camera was small, a person would have to look closely to see it. Susie herself had trouble seeing it.

She found a clump of bushes and hid in them. From her cramped position, she glanced at her watch and saw that it was 2:09. She had made it with 6 minutes to spare. Susie had to sit very quietly without making a sound. She peered through the dense leaves and thin, zigzagged branches. Susie sat in her position very silently… waiting for the prime minister and Timothy Robins.

Chapter 17

Now it was 2:11…2:12…2:13… At 2:14, Susie heard footsteps and made sure that she was not visible. The prime minister, Zachary Whitley, came into view. He looked around and pressed his fingers together. A few moments later, Timothy Robins came up to the prime minister.

Susie suddenly thought of something that she had not given much thought to earlier. She realized that the prime minister had led her to ask Robins about the alarm system. If she had gone to another repairman, her movements would not have been watched. Did Robins watch as she entered the tunnels, wait a few seconds, then follow her? He was heavy and had blue eyes, so it could have been him. However, Timothy Robins was not wearing a guard's uniform. Was a guard also involved in the thefts, and just the prime minister and Robins were meeting? Would a guard show up?

"I did not see that girl in the hallway anymore," began the prime minister. "However, I am not concerned as she has no idea we are behind the thefts. She is probably wandering around the palace right now." Susie smiled at this. He had no idea she was hiding right there, listening to their conversation and recording it!

"As for the Final Project," began Robins, "We should best get it done and out of the way. Trammer is waiting for us to give her the valuables from our recent thefts and our future Final Project."

The prime minister replied, "All in good time, Timothy. That girl does not know that the painting we stole is hidden under the couch in the same room it was stolen from. She didn't even check the crime scene! As for the Golden Goblet, we must remove it from inside the vase in the parlor. An obvious hiding place that she didn't even think of checking. And the sapphire was in the drawer with the note I left for you!"

Robins asked, "Why did you even ask her to come to solve the mystery?".

"Because it is part of my job, and I don't want anyone to suspect me. Besides, Susie is only twelve and won't ever think of me as a thief. I made it seem as though I was being set up!" Whitley replied.

Susie began to think. Samuel Hardie might have taken the painting down. Then, he hid it in the same room. Afterward, he made a loud racket and lay on the floor with the rug, pretending that the carpet had been thrown at him. The figure in the dark room was to serve as a distraction, maybe.

"I took the silver bracelet from the room next to my office while pretending to look for some papers. In my office, I quickly tore the seams of a pillow out and placed the bracelet inside. Then, I sewed it back together and placed it in a sitting room a few hours ago.", the prime minister said. "While the ball is in progress, we will steal the jewel-encrusted gold statue. It will be heavy, and we will steal it during the ball, so the loud music will drown out the noise of us stealing it. We will take it outside into the garden and give it to Trammer to load into her freight truck that she will keep hidden behind the trees. Then, we will return to the palace and bring out the sapphire, painting, bracelet, and goblet. Who would suspect us when we carry out a pillow and a vase if anyone does happen to see us? And the sapphire will be in my pocket. We will take great care in removing the painting Samuel stole, which will be done last because its canvas is fragile and the frame is heavy.", the prime minister said.

Listening to their conversation, Susie thought that they were being very open with each other. They were so sure that they would succeed! Susie also wondered who Trammer was and if a guard or the butler was involved. Trammer was probably part of the group of thieves. Susie also wondered what bracelet the prime minister was speaking of. She knew that she would find out soon. Susie would record the entire crime without them knowing. Susie also had one problem she needed to resolve: She would be recording; however, once everything was loaded into the truck, Trammer would drive off - and the valuables would be gone.

"I cannot wait until our Final Project is over. Then, I can finish my part-time job at the palace. Can't drop out just after the thefts, or I'll be suspected.", Timothy Robins put in.

The prime minister told Susie he had just started working at the palace. He was most likely only working there so he could pull off the thefts. He would probably resign after the heist.

"We're all set, and I don't want this meeting to be longer than necessary. I was sent to fix some shingles on the palace roof, and everyone thinks that's what I am doing.", Robins concluded. "And that girl may notice that we are missing."

Susie certainly knew where they were!

And this was the end of the meeting. Susie watched as the two men set off toward the palace. She began to plan something. She could tell the prime minister that she was done looking into the thefts and would only attend the ball for the fun of it. Really, Susie was not giving up.

She was going to say that she was done so that the two thieves would think she was no longer after them, which would make them feel more at ease. As soon as the thieves' footsteps faded away, Susie stood up, grabbed her camera, and ended the recording. Susie started to walk up to the palace.

As soon as she entered, she searched the palace so she would know where all the valuables would be. One thing: she could say who the thieves were and locate the valuables, but she needed evidence to succeed in closing the case. Susie also wondered if a guard or the butler was helping in the Final Project. Neither had attended the meeting by the cave, but that didn't mean they were not accomplices.

Susie felt all the pillows in various sitting rooms until she located the one with the bracelet. Susie also found the painting under the couch. Additionally, Susie located the golden statue. Finally, she found the Golden Goblet inside a vase in the sitting room. Susie already knew where the sapphire was - locked inside the prime minister's desk drawer.

Afterward, Susie went into the prime minister's office. Whitley was sitting at his desk.

"I have come here to tell you that I do not believe any more thefts will occur. As for the past thefts, I simply do not know how they took place or how to recover the stolen items. I would suggest that you hire an investigation team." Really, it was just a cover. Susie was determined to not give up.

Susie thought she saw a quick smile flash across the prime minister's face, which proved that he was pleased she was done working on the case. This meant the thieves would not need to be careful keeping an eye on her. Therefore, it would make it easier for Susie as she would know that no one would be looking for her.

The prime minister tapped his fingers together. "That is alright. At least you tried. However, I invite you to the big ball at 6:00 PM." If the prime minister invited her to be present during the thefts, he must be confident that he and the other thieves would get away!

"Thank you." And with that, Susie walked out of the palace.

Chapter 18

When she got home, she retrieved several small cameras. One would be pinned into her hair, so she could record the thefts from where she was. She had four other small cameras. One would be in the sitting room with the bracelet, another with the statue, another facing the locked drawer of the prime minister's desk, and the last in the room where the painting was hidden.

Susie additionally took a larger camera. The thieves' truck would be hidden behind some trees in the garden. Susie would discreetly put the camera up to face where the truck would be to record it.

Finally, Susie took out a tape recorder. She would hide it near where she suspected the truck would be parked to record additional audio that her cameras would be unable to capture. Susie knew it was necessary to arrive early to get everything set up before the ball. She also must hide the cameras and tape recorder in a way so that the thieves would not know that she would be recording them.

At 5:30 PM, Susie put on a lovely dress. It was dark blue, with pink embroidery and white lace. She also put the cameras and tape recorder into a handbag, so no one would see her carrying them. She pulled up her hair and put on a hairband with large rhinestones. She slid the small camera into her hair where it would not be visible.

Susie ran into the living room and pulled out a flat screen. Everything recorded with the miniature cameras would go to this screen, where they could be viewed. She wanted to be careful with it. She placed it on a shelf behind several books. The thieves knew where she lived; if they were suspicious, they could always break in and steal the screen. That way, although she would be recording, she would be unable to access her recordings. And she would be the only witness of the final thefts.

At 5:43, Susie walked into the palace. In the parlor where the Golden Goblet was, Susie hung a camera. In the room with the painting, Susie positioned another camera. Susie placed a camera in the prime minister's office, focused on the drawer. Additionally, Susie hung a camera in the room with the golden statue. Lastly, in the room with the bracelet, Susie hid a camera focused on the pillow.

Then, Susie went outside into the garden. Near the place where the truck would be, Susie placed the tape recorder in a pile of leaves. Afterward, Susie climbed one of the trees and strapped the large camera around the trunk. Using a string, she tied back some branches so the camera could record the theft without the tree obscuring the view.

Susie was able to get all of these cameras in place because Robins and the prime minister were in the ballroom, helping to set up.

There was still one camera in Susie's handbag. It was the one she had used to record the thieves' meeting. It was running out of storage, so she would only turn it on while recording the thieves.

Susie's plan was to leave the ballroom after one of the thieves saw her in it, making them believe that she would do no further investigating. There would be many people, so no one would notice if she left after one minute.

Chapter 19

At 6:00, Susie entered the ballroom, saw the prime minister, and waved to him. Now one of the thieves would think she would be at the ball. She pretended to talk to someone and watched out of the corner of her eye as the prime minister and Timothy Robins walked out of the ballroom. Susie counted to ten, then followed them out very quietly. She turned on her hand camera and recorded the two thieves entering the room with the statue. Susie hid under a table in the hallway. A few minutes later, the two thieves staggered out with the heavy statue as Susie recorded them. After they went around a bend in the hallway, Susie got up and followed them. Once outside, the thieves approached a truck behind some trees in the garden.

"Hurry up, you two," a voice said near a truck. It was female. Perhaps it was Trammer, and that was her last name.

Susie crouched behind some bushes and recorded as the prime minister and Robins loaded the statue into the back of the truck. Then, they returned to the palace for the smaller items. Susie knew that it would be useless to follow them. They would split up and go into many different rooms and collect all of the small goods simultaneously, and Susie had already prepared cameras. Susie decided to stay near the truck and continue to record. Trammer stood near the back of the truck, tapping her foot impatiently. It seemed like she was the leader of the ring of thieves.

Suddenly, Susie thought that her plan had a small problem. Once all the valuables were stolen, then the truck would drive off, and the valuables would be sold for lots of money. After Robins and Whitley finished working at the palace, they would leave and disappear forever.

Suddenly, Susie looked at Trammer and remembered the reporter she had called earlier: Caroline Tram. Her image in the newspaper looked very similar to Trammer. Maybe Caroline Tram was Trammer! And she knew of the thefts because she had helped with them. And she published it! This way, she would not be suspected! She would not reveal her sources because the sources were thieves. Susie reminded herself to think of this later – she needed to solve the current problem.

The prime minister and Robins had come back with the small valuables after about a minute. Now they would go back for the painting. Trammer said she would go with them and look for any other valuables that could be stolen that night.

As they left, Susie saw her chance. She would not go after them to record. The camera in the room with the painting would record them taking it.

Susie has a plan. She climbed up into the front of the truck. She searched for a sharp object. Nothing there. Then, she checked the back. Not only was it full of the things stolen from the palace, but it contained many other valuables! These were thieves who stole from many places. Susie made sure that she had recorded all that was inside. Then, she searched for a sharp object. There was still nothing! Susie searched near the fountain in the garden and located a nail in the ground. She was not sure why it was there, but it would work. She would use it to pierce the tires of the truck. Then, the thieves could not drive away.

She ran back to the truck and slashed all four tires very well. Now, she needed to find a way to catch the thieves.

Susie looked towards the door that opened up into the garden. The thieves were approaching! Luckily, the painting was heavy. Caroline Tram carried a sack in her hand and was helping to guide Timothy Robins and the prime minister. She needed to hurry and get a trap set. Susie made herself think.

The thieves were about 700 yards away and could not see her yet. Then, she had an idea. She dived into a bush and was quiet. The thieves came up and loaded the painting into the back of the truck, along with the sack that Caroline was carrying. All the while, Susie recorded from the bush.

Suddenly, Robins gasped. He had noticed that all the tires were slashed.

"The tires have been slashed!" he exclaimed.

"How are we going to get to the Windbrier Museum to steal the helmet of Prince George and the collection of rare coins now?" Trammer said in an exasperated tone.

"I know who did it!" said the prime minister. "It is that girl, Susie. She lied when she said that she had given up."

Susie stood up from the bush and said, "It is also dishonest to steal, and I see you have stolen from many places!"

Chapter 20

She heard one of the thieves shout and began to run into the woods, as this was part of her plan. She heard running footsteps pursue her. Susie ran as fast as she could. Her goal was to lead the thieves to the abandoned structure she had found on her way to the meeting place. Susie ran as fast as she could and veered off from the paved path onto the overgrown path from before. She ran until she found the structure. Then, she ran inside.

Susie knew the floor was falling in, so she carefully crossed the structure until she reached the side opposite the door, where the floor was firmer. The thieves soon entered.

"We have you cornered, and we will not allow you to interfere with our thefts.", said

Trammer, whom Susie presumed was Caroline Tram.

"What should we do?" wondered Robins. "We do not want her to tell others about our thefts."

Susie interjected. "Before you begin your negotiation, could you clarify some things for me?" When none of the thieves said anything, Susie began asking questions. She placed her hand camera in her pocket, not wanting the thieves to know she was recording them. Susie knew the camera she had hidden in her hair would capture everything that was about to happen.

"Who stole the Golden Goblet?"
"Samuel Hardie," said the prime minister.
"Is the butler involved in any way?"
"No, but while he was king, he did mastermind the bank theft. I was part of the group who stole the money", said Timothy Robins.

"When the painting was stolen, did Hardie hide it in the same room?"

"Yes, he did, under the couch, and then he put on the act of being knocked down. The man in the cloak you chased was me. I did that to distract you. I thought throwing the curtain at you would make you scared, so you would stop looking into what was going on.", Timothy Robins explained.

"Was the coin significant to anything?"

The prime minister said, "We left it there to make you believe that the butler was the thief.'

"Why did you even ask me to solve the case?"

The prime minister said, "Because, as a part of my job, if something happens, I am responsible for finding someone to help resolve it. And we thought that it would be fun to see if a twelve-year-old could catch us. We did not intend it to go this way."

"Why was the cloak hanging in your office?"

"To make you believe that I was being set up.", The prime minister explained.
"Who was chasing me in the tunnels? What were they doing down there?"
"It was me. After I examined the alarm system for you, which I had cut just then, I ran into the closet next to the vault. There, I put on a guard's uniform and covered my head with fabric. Once I found that you had discovered the tunnels, I followed you to scare you. Then, I trapped you inside the tunnels because I assumed you were following me. I have no idea how you got out.", Robins said.
"Who stole the China?" Susie asked.
"Samuel Hardie. He turned off the electricity, entered the kitchen, and carefully unlocked the cabinet using my key, " said the prime minister.
"Is Trammer, Caroline Tram? Did you publish your own theft?"
Trammer said, "Yes to both questions."
"Are you three the only thieves other than Hardie?"

"Yes," Caroline, Robins, and the prime minister said in unison.

"Who stole the sapphire? Did you use the tunnels?"

"I did, and yes, I used the tunnels.", the prime minister said.

"What other places have you robbed?"

"Many places. We have been stealing for years, but no one has been able to catch us. And no one *will*.", Caroline said.

The thieves were getting closer. They paid no attention to the floor sagging under their weight. All of a sudden, the floor collapsed!

Chapter 21

Susie had planned this all along. When the floor collapsed, the thieves fell into the empty basement far below. There were no stairs, so they were stuck down there. The entire floor had given in, except for the part where Susie was standing. She knew from the start that this section of the floor where she stood was stable and would not give in.

Now, she needed to find a way out of the structure to get the guards. Luckily, the building was falling apart. Susie simply pushed out the wall behind her and climbed out of the abandoned structure.

Immediately, Susie ran to the palace and explained what had happened to the guards. Five went to the structure to arrest the thieves.

The butler, standing nearby, had heard all that had happened. He was aware that Susie knew he had masterminded the bank theft as king. He turned and ran, only to be caught by two of the palace guards.

"Just one question for you.", Susie began. "Did you steal anything recently?" Susie was sure he had not but just wanted to verify what the other thieves had said.

"No," the butler replied.

"One more thing: Why was your hair pressed down yesterday? I thought you were the thief and had worn a piece of fabric over your head to steal some valuables."

"My hair was pressed down because I wore a hat to go outside on my break. I went into the bathroom to fix it later."

After five minutes, one of the guards returned and said all three thieves claimed they were innocent. The prime minister and Robins said they had seen Susie running into the woods and thought she was after something. They followed to help. They stated that Susie had entered the structure and that they had merely followed her. Caroline Tram had come to attend the ball and wanted to ask the prime minister some questions for her upcoming publication in the newspaper. When she saw Robins and the prime minister run into the woods, she thought there might be a good story to publish the following day.

"This is not true.", Susie said. "I recorded everything."

Susie went about and collected all the cameras and the tape recorder. She handed them over to the guard, along with her hand camera and the camera that had been in her hair. They had the perfect evidence.

The guard left to put the evidence in a safe place. Another guard arrived and said that the thieves had dropped their cover and told of every theft they had pulled off.

Finally, she had caught all of the thieves! Susie could not wait for another mystery to solve…

About the Author

The author, 12-year-old Skye Oduaran, is a 6th grader who enjoys reading, writing, running, and playing the flute. At age 11, Skye was one of only 29 kids worldwide to be selected as a kid journalist for Scholastic Kids Press. She has covered numerous political events at the state and national levels. Skye covered the Georgia gubernatorial and senate elections, meeting prominent figures, including President Barack Obama. She has interviewed Governor Brian Kemp, Senator Raphael Warnock, former United Nations ambassador Andrew Young, and State Rep. Stacey Abrams, among many others. In the fall of 2022, Skye covered President Biden's Pardoning of the Thanksgiving Turkeys, Chocolate & Chip, from the White House. She has recently interviewed actresses America Ferrera, Tessa Thompson, and Poet Laurette Ada Limón.

Made in the USA
Columbia, SC
17 April 2023